MARC and PIXIE

Also by Louise Fatio and illustrated by Roger Duvoisin

THE HAPPY LION

THE HAPPY LION IN AFRICA

THE HAPPY LION AND THE BEAR

THE HAPPY LION ROARS

THE HAPPY LION'S QUEST

THE HAPPY LION'S TREASURE

THE HAPPY LION'S VACATION

THE THREE HAPPY LIONS

THE HAPPY LION'S RABBITS

RED BANTAM

HECTOR PENGUIN

MARC and PIXIE

and the walls in Mrs. Jones's garden

by Louise Fatio and Roger Duvoisin

McGraw-Hill Book Company

New York   St. Louis   San Francisco   Düsseldorf   Johannesburg
Kuala Lumpur   London   Mexico   Montreal   New Delhi   Panama
Paris   São Paulo   Singapore   Sydney   Tokyo   Toronto

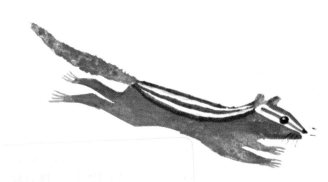

To our piece of a beautiful countryside
and its wildlife

Library of Congress Cataloging in Publication Data

Fatio, Louise.
  Marc and Pixie, and the walls in Mrs. Jones's
garden.

  SUMMARY: The Siamese cat changes the atmosphere,
especially for a fat chipmunk, in the Jones's happy
garden.
  I. Duvoisin, Roger Antoine,   joint author.
II. Title.
PZ7.F268Mar   [E]   75-14194
ISBN 0-07-020038-6
ISBN 0-07-020039-4 lib. bdg.

Copyright © 1975 by Louise Fatio and Roger Duvoisin. All Rights Reserved. Printed in the United States of
America. No part of this publication may be reproduced, stored in a retrieval system, or transmitted, in any
form or by any means, electronic, mechanical, photocopying, recording, or otherwise, without the prior
written permission of the publisher.

34567RABP789876

Mr. Angelo loved stones, flat-faced stones, shaped just right to build stone walls. Mr. Angelo also loved to build stone walls in Mrs. Jones's garden with just the right flat-faced stones.

Mr. Angelo loved to build walls more than caring for flowers, and that is why he built so many stone walls in Mrs. Jones's garden. He built walls in the courtyard; walls along the rain ditches; walls along the vegetable garden; walls beside the pond; walls here, walls there, walls everywhere! Mr. Angelo could not stop building walls.

Mrs. Jones loved the walls that Mr. Angelo built and she said, "Mr. Angelo, you are the best stone-wall builder in the world."

"Thank you, Mrs. Jones," answered Mr. Angelo. He agreed he was.

Now, if Mr. Angelo loved to build walls with just the right flat-faced stones; if Mrs. Jones loved the walls that Mr. Angelo built; Marc the chipmunk loved the holes between the flat-faced stones of the walls that Mr. Angelo built. He loved them because they made just the right sort of entrance to the burrows he dug behind the stones.

So, Marc came to live in Mr. Angelo's walls with his wife and children and sisters and brothers and cousins and uncles and aunts and nephews and nieces and grandfather and grandmother and

great-uncles and great-aunts and friends.

And the walls in Mrs. Jones's garden became a city of chipmunks. It was a happy city. Until...

...until one day, Mrs. Jones bought a Siamese cat named Pixie.

Now, if Mr. Angelo loved to build walls in Mrs. Jones's garden; if Mrs. Jones loved the walls Mr. Angelo built; if Marc the chipmunk and his family and friends loved the holes between the flat-faced stones of Mr. Angelo's walls; Pixie the Siamese cat loved the chipmunks who lived in the walls.

Alas, she loved them because she wanted to eat them. *They must be even more delicious than mice,* she thought. Most of all, she wanted to eat Marc, who was the fattest of the family.

Sadly for Pixie, Mr. Angelo's walls had many holes. The chipmunks slipped in and out of them so fast, Pixie could never catch any.

NEVER?

One night, Mrs. Jones was awakened by Pixie's meows. Pixie had climbed the trumpet vine to the window and wanted to be let in. Mrs. Jones went and opened the window. Pixie jumped down to the floor with a chipmunk in her mouth.

It was Marc.

"Pixie!" cried Mrs. Jones, "You nasty cat! Let this chipmunk go!"

Pixie opened her mouth in surprise and Marc escaped under the bed.   He was not hurt.

Pixie ran after him.

Mrs. Jones who loved chipmunks crept after Pixie.

Mr. Jones who loved what Mrs. Jones loved crept after her to help.

The bedroom chase was on!

Marc ran into the chest of drawers, into the clothes closet, under the bed pillows and blankets, over the dressing table— under, over and into everything in the bedroom. Pixie ran after

Marc, Mrs. Jones ran after Pixie, Mr. Jones ran after Mrs. Jones.
It was as if an earthquake had hit the bedroom.

Suddenly, having had enough, Pixie jumped out the window. Marc, exhausted, fell asleep in the wastebasket. Mr. and Mrs. Jones went back to bed.   The chase was over.

The next morning, Mrs. Jones took Marc out of the waste-basket. She laid him on a bed of soft cotton in the old canary cage and gave him a dish of hazelnuts. Marc was still dazed.

Mr. Jones found Pixie crying in the flower bed under the bedroom window. She had broken a leg in her fall. Mr. Jones took
her to the veterinarian who put her leg into a plaster-cast.

Later that day, Pixie lay on the living-room couch looking sadly at Marc. Marc looked sleepily at Pixie from the canary cage.

For days, Pixie looked at Marc; Marc looked at Pixie. Little
by little they began to like the looks of each other.

When Marc was well enough to be let out of the canary cage, he went closer and closer to Pixie-in-the-plaster-cast. Finally he said, "Hello! How are you?"

Pixie answered, "Hello, I don't feel too good. I can't walk."

Mrs. Jones brought Pixie a dish of milk and Marc climbed onto the couch. He said, "Hello, I like your soft fur," and began to lap up the milk.

Pixie said, "Hello, I like your bright little eyes."

Both lapped the milk together.

The next day Marc said, "Pixie, when you can walk again we will lie together in the sun."

"Yes, Marc, I would love it. I hope it will be soon."

And this is how Pixie began to love not only Marc, but all the chipmunks who lived in the walls that Mr. Angelo built.

In Mrs. Jones's garden anyone can now see Pixie sitting happily with Marc, while all around them Marc's wife and children

and mother and father and grandmother and grandfather and aunts and uncles and nephews and nieces and great-aunts and great-uncles and cousins and friends go in and out of the holes in Mr. Angelo's wall.

So, the walls that Mr. Angelo built in Mrs. Jones's garden brought joy to everyone—to Mr. Angelo, to Mrs. Jones and Mr. Jones, to Pixie, and to Marc and his family and friends.

And Mr. Angelo went on building walls with just the right flat-faced stones in Mrs. Jones's garden.